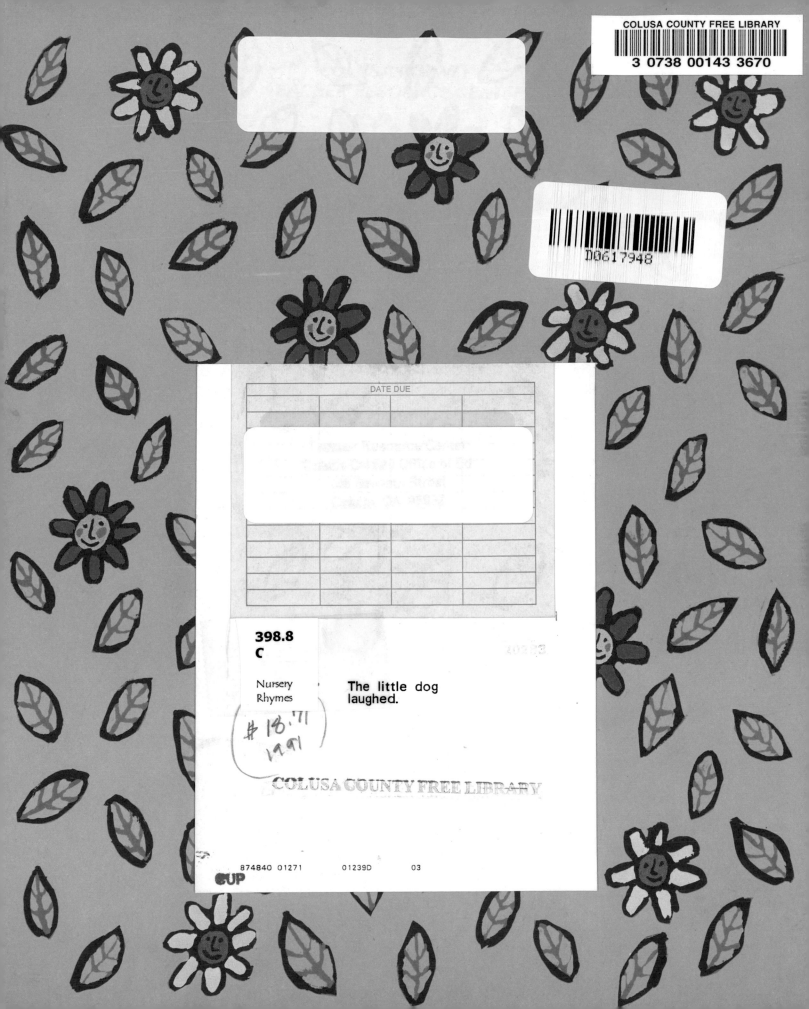

The little dog laughed

Lucy Cousins

E. P. Dutton · New York

Contents

for Oonagh

First published in the United States 1990 by E. P. Dutton,
a division of Penguin Books USA Inc.

Originally published in 1989 by
Macmillan Children's Books
4 Little Essex Street, London WC2R 3LF

The rhymes in this book are reprinted from
The Oxford Nursery Rhyme Book, assembled
by Iona and Peter Opie (1955) by permission of
Oxford University Press.

First American Edition   Printed in Belgium
ISBN 0-525-44573-0   10 9 8 7 6 5 4 3 2 1

to
see a
fine
lady

upon
a
white
horse

Ride a cockhorse to Banbury Cross,
To see a fine lady upon a white horse;
Rings on her fingers and bells on her toes,
And she shall have music wherever she goes.

humpty dumpty sat on a wall

Humpty Dumpty sat on a wall,
Humpty Dumpty had a great fall;
All the King's horses and all the King's men
Couldn't put Humpty together again.

Oranges and lemons,
Say the bells of St. Clement's.

You owe me five farthings,
Say the bells of St. Martin's.

When will you pay me?
Say the bells at Old Bailey.

When I grow rich,
Say the bells at Shoreditch.

When will that be?
Say the bells at Stepney.

I'm sure I don't know,
Says the great bell at Bow.

Here comes a candle to light you to bed,
Here comes a chopper to chop off your head.

Oranges
and
lemons

One, two, three, four, five,
I caught a fish alive
Six, seven, eight, nine, ten,
I let it go again.
Why did you let it go?
Because it bit my finger so.
Which finger did it bite?
The little finger on the right.

Baa, baa, black sheep,
    Have you any wool?
Yes sir, yes sir,
    Three bags full;
One for the master,
    And one for the dame,
And one for the little boy
    Who lives down the lane.

baa baa black sheep

Jack and Jill
Went up the hill,
To fetch a pail of water;
Jack fell down,
And broke his crown,
And Jill came tumbling after.

Then up Jack got,
And home did trot,
As fast as he could caper;
To old Dame Dob,
Who patched his nob
With vinegar and brown paper.

When Jill came in,
How she did grin
To see Jack's paper plaster,
Her mother, vexed,
Did whip her next,
For laughing at Jack's disaster.

Now Jack did laugh
And Jill did cry,
But her tears did soon abate;
Then Jill did say
That they should play
At seesaw across the gate.

11

Bow-wow, says the dog,
Mew, mew, says the cat,
Grunt, grunt, goes the hog,
And squeak goes the rat.
Tu, whu, says the owl,
Caw, caw, says the crow,
Quack, quack, says the duck,
And what cuckoos say you know.

12

I had a little nut tree,
　　Nothing would it bear
But a silver nutmeg
　　And a golden pear;
The King of Spain's daughter
　　Came to visit me,
And all for the sake
　　Of my little nut tree.
I skipped over water,
　　I danced over sea,
And all the birds in the air
　　Couldn't catch me.

Tom Tom

Tom, Tom, the piper's son,
Stole a pig and away he run;
The pig was eat,
And Tom was beat,
And Tom went howling down the street.

Cobbler cobbler

Cobbler, cobbler, mend my shoe,
Get it done by half past two;
Stitch it up, and stitch it down,
Then I'll give you half a crown.

there was a crooked man

There was a crooked man,
    And he walked a crooked mile;
He found a crooked sixpence
    Against a crooked stile;
He bought a crooked cat,
    Which caught a crooked mouse,
And they all lived together
    In a little crooked house.

I saw three ships come sailing in,
  Come sailing in, come sailing in,
I saw three ships come sailing in,
  On Christmas day in the morning.

And what do you think was in them then,
  Was in them then, was in them then?
And what do you think was in them then,
  On Christmas day in the morning?

Three pretty girls were in them then,
    Were in them then, were in them then,
Three pretty girls were in them then,
    On Christmas day in the morning.

One could whistle, and one could sing,
    And one could play on the violin;
Such joy there was at my wedding,
    On Christmas day in the morning.

I saw three ships

Two little dicky birds,
Sitting on a wall;
One named Peter,
The other named Paul.
Fly away, Peter!
Fly away, Paul!
Come back, Peter!
Come back, Paul!

two little
dicky
birds

Polly
put
the
kettle
on

Polly put the kettle on,
Polly put the kettle on,
Polly put the kettle on,
We'll all have tea.

Sukey take it off again,
Sukey take it off again,
Sukey take it off again,
They've all gone away.

Goosey, goosey gander,
  Whither shall I wander?
Upstairs and downstairs
  And in my lady's chamber.
There I met an old man
  Who would not say his prayers,
I took him by the left leg
  And threw him down the stairs.

Oh, the brave old Duke of York,
    He had ten thousand men;
He marched them up to the top of the hill,
    And he marched them down again.
And when they were up, they were up,
    And when they were down, they were down,
And when they were only halfway up,
    They were neither up nor down.

the
brave
old
duke
of
York

I had a little horse,
　　His name was Dapple Gray,
His head was made of gingerbread,
　　His tail was made of hay.
He could amble, he could trot,
　　He could carry the mustard pot.
He could amble, he could trot,
　　Through the old town of Windsor.

22

rain
rain

Rain, rain, go away,
Come again another day,
Little Johnny wants to play.

Willie
Wilkin

Long
Daniel

Betty
Bodkin

Little
Dick

Tom
Thumbkin

Tom Thumbkin,
Willie Wilkin,
Long Daniel,
Betty Bodkin,
And Little Dick.

the Queen of hearts she made some tarts

The Queen of Hearts
She made some tarts,
All on a summer's day;
The Knave of Hearts
He stole those tarts,
And took them clean away.

The King of Hearts
Called for the tarts,
And beat the knave full sore;
The Knave of Hearts
Brought back the tarts,
And vowed he'd steal no more.

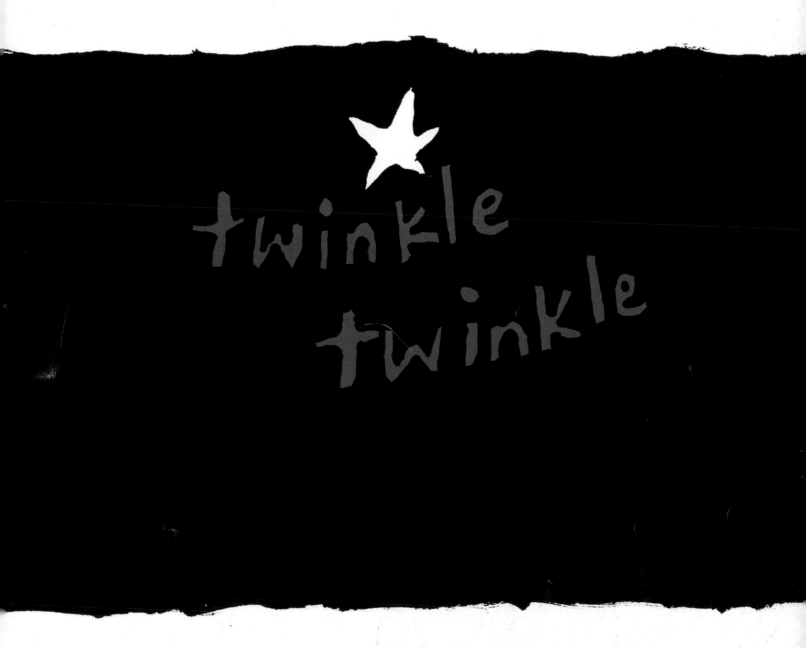

twinkle twinkle

Twinkle, twinkle, little star,
How I wonder what you are!
Up above the world so high,
Like a diamond in the sky.

Simple Simon met a pieman,
   Going to the fair;
Said Simple Simon to the pieman,
   "Let me taste your ware."

Said the pieman to Simple Simon,
   "Show me first your penny."
Said Simple Simon to the pieman,
   "Indeed I have not any."

Simple Simon went a-fishing,
   For to catch a whale;
All the water he had got
   Was in his mother's pail.

Simple Simon went to look
   If plums grew on a thistle;
He pricked his fingers very much,
   Which made poor Simon whistle.

He went for water in a sieve
   But soon it all fell through;
And now poor Simple Simon
   Bids you all adieu.

26

Dance to your daddy,
My little baby,
Dance to your daddy,
My little lamb.

You shall have a fishy
In a little dishy,
You shall have a fishy
When the boat comes in.

You shall have an apple,
You shall have a plum,
You shall have a rattle
When your daddy comes home.

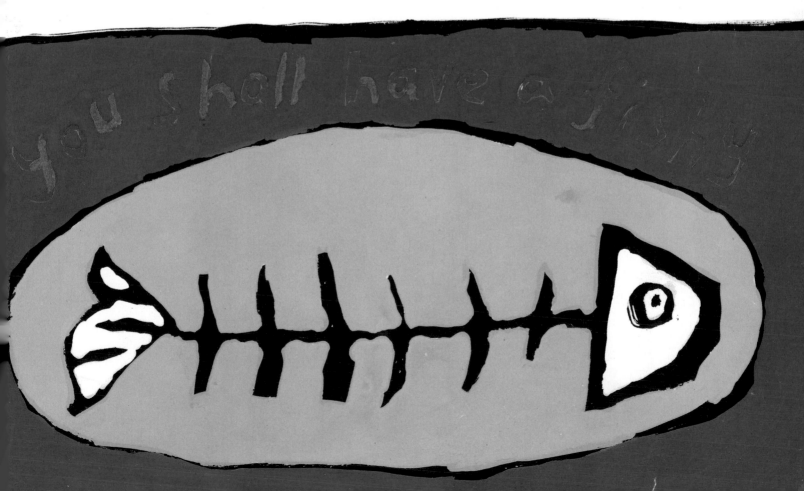

One, two, Buckle my shoe

Three, four, knock on the door;

Five, six, pick up sticks;

Seven, eight, lay them straight;

Nine, ten, a big fat hen;
Eleven, twelve, dig and delve;
Thirteen, fourteen, maids a-courting;
Fifteen, sixteen, maids in the kitchen;
Seventeen, eighteen, maids in waiting;
Nineteen, twenty, my plate's empty.

3
blind
mice

Three blind mice, see how they run!
They all ran after the farmer's wife,
Who cut off their tails with a carving knife,
Did you ever see such a sight in your life
As three blind mice?

Mary, Mary, quite contrary,
How does your garden grow?
With silver bells and cockleshells,
And pretty maids all in a row.

The lion and the unicorn
    Were fighting for the crown;
The lion beat the unicorn
    All around the town.

Some gave them white bread,
    And some gave them brown;
Some gave them plum cake
    And drummed them out of town.

Old Mother Hubbard
Went to the cupboard,
To fetch her poor dog a bone;
But when she got there,
The cupboard was bare,
And so the poor dog had none.

She went to the baker's
To buy him some bread;
But when she came back,
The poor dog was dead.

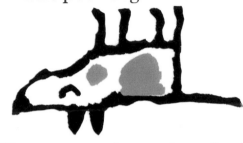

She went to the undertaker's
To buy him a coffin;
But when she came back,
The poor dog was laughing.

She took a clean dish
To get him some tripe;
But when she came back,
He was smoking a pipe.

She went to the tavern
For white wine and red;
But when she came back,
The dog stood on his head.

She went to the grocer's
To buy him some fruit;
But when she came back,
He was playing the flute.

She went to the tailor's
To buy him a coat;
But when she came back,
He was riding a goat.

She went to the hatter's
To buy him a hat;
But when she came back,
He was feeding the cat.

old mother hubbard

She went to the barber's
 To buy him a wig;
But when she came back,
 He was dancing a jig.

She went to the cobbler's
 To buy him some shoes;
But when she came back,
 He was reading the news.

She went to the hosier's
 To buy him some hose;
But when she came back,
 He was dressed in his clothes.

The dame made a curtsy,
 The dog made a bow;
The dame said, "Your servant,"
 The dog said, "Bow-wow."

bow
wow

One, two, three, four,
Mary's at the cottage door,
Five, six, seven, eight,
Eating cherries off a plate.

cock
a
doodle
doo

Cock-a-doodle-doo!
My dame has lost her shoe,
My master's lost his fiddling stick
And knows not what to do.

Cock-a-doodle-doo!
What is my dame to do?
Till master finds his fiddling stick
She'll dance without her shoe.

Cock-a-doodle-doo!
My dame has found her shoe,
And master's found his fiddling stick,
Sing doodle doodle doo.

Cock-a-doodle-doo!
My dame will dance with you,
While master fiddles his fiddling stick
For dame and doodle doo.

Hot cross buns! Hot cross buns!
One a penny, two a penny,
Hot cross buns!
If your daughters do not like them
Give them to your sons;
And if you have not any of these pretty little elves,
You cannot do better than eat them yourselves.

lady bug
lady
bug

Ladybug, ladybug,
 Fly away home,
Your house is on fire
 And your children all gone;
All except one
 And that's little Ann,
And she has crept under
 The warming pan.

The eensy, weensy spider
    Went up the waterspout;
Down came the rain
    And washed the spider out.
Out came the sun
    And dried up all the rain;
And the eensy, weensy spider
    Went up the spout again.

Grandfa' Grig
Had a pig,
In a field of clover;
Piggy died,
Grandfa' cried,
And all the fun was over.

Grandfa' Grig
had
a
pig

There was an old woman who lived in a shoe,
She had so many children she didn't know what to do;
She gave them some broth without any bread;
She whipped them all soundly and put them to bed.

there was
an old
Woman

Old King Cole
Was a merry old soul,
And a merry old soul was he;
He called for his pipe,
And he called for his bowl,
And he called for his fiddlers three.

Every fiddler he had a fiddle,
And a very fine fiddle had he;
Oh, there's none so rare
As can compare
With King Cole and his fiddlers three.

Mary had a little lamb,
   Its fleece was white as snow,
And everywhere that Mary went
   The lamb was sure to go.

It followed her to school one day,
   That was against the rule,
It made the children laugh and play
   To see a lamb at school.

And so the teacher turned it out,
   But still it lingered near;
And waited patiently about
   Till Mary did appear.

"Why does the lamb love Mary so?"
   The eager children cry;
"Why, Mary loves the lamb, you know,"
   The teacher did reply.

mary
had a
little
lamb

On the first day of Christmas
My true love sent to me
A partridge in a pear tree.

On the second day of Christmas
My true love sent to me
Two turtledoves, and
A partridge in a pear tree.

On the third day of Christmas
My true love sent to me
Three French hens,
Two turtledoves, and
A partridge in a pear tree.

On the fourth day of Christmas
My true love sent to me
Four calling birds,
Three French hens,
Two turtledoves, and
A partridge in a pear tree.

On the fifth day of Christmas
My true love sent to me
Five golden rings,
Four calling birds,
Three French hens,
Two turtledoves, and
A partridge in a pear tree.

On the sixth day of Christmas
My true love sent to me
Six geese a-laying,
Five golden rings,
Four calling birds,
Three French hens,
Two turtledoves, and
A partridge in a pear tree.

On the seventh day of Christmas
My true love sent to me
Seven swans a-swimming,
Six geese a-laying,
Five golden rings,
Four calling birds,
Three French hens,
Two turtledoves, and
A partridge in a pear tree.

On the eighth day of Christmas
My true love sent to me
Eight maids a-milking,
Seven swans a-swimming,
Six geese a-laying,
Five golden rings,
Four calling birds,
Three French hens,
Two turtledoves, and
A partridge in a pear tree.

On the ninth day of Christmas
My true love sent to me
Nine drummers drumming,
Eight maids a-milking,
Seven swans a-swimming,
Six geese a-laying,
Five golden rings,
Four calling birds,
Three French hens,
Two turtledoves, and
A partridge in a pear tree.

On the tenth day of Christmas
My true love sent to me
Ten pipers piping,
Nine drummers drumming,
Eight maids a-milking,
Seven swans a-swimming,
Six geese a-laying,
Five golden rings,
Four calling birds,
Three French hens,
Two turtledoves, and
A partridge in a pear tree.

On the eleventh day of Christmas
My true love sent to me
Eleven ladies dancing,
Ten pipers piping,
Nine drummers drumming,
Eight maids a-milking,
Seven swans a-swimming,
Six geese a-laying,
Five golden rings,
Four calling birds,
Three French hens,
Two turtledoves, and
A partridge in a pear tree.

On the twelfth day of Christmas
My true love sent to me
Twelve lords a-leaping,
Eleven ladies dancing,
Ten pipers piping,
Nine drummers drumming,
Eight maids a-milking,
Seven swans a-swimming,
Six geese a-laying,
Five golden rings,
Four calling birds,
Three French hens,
Two turtledoves, and
A partridge in a pear tree.

Hickory, dickory, dock,
The mouse ran up the clock.
  The clock struck one,
  The mouse ran down,
Hickory, dickory, dock.

47

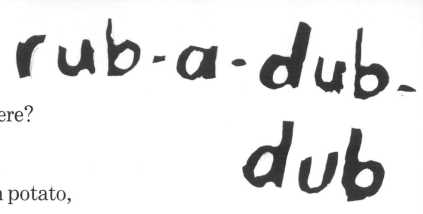

rub-a-dub-
dub

Rub-a-dub-dub,
Three men in a tub,
And how do you think they got there?
The butcher, the baker,
The candlestick maker,
They all jumped out of a rotten potato,
'Twas enough to make a man stare.

The north wind doth blow,
And we shall have snow,
And what will poor Robin do then?
    Poor thing.
He'll sit in a barn,
And keep himself warm,
And hide his head under his wing,
    Poor thing.

Hey diddle, diddle,
The cat and the fiddle,
The cow jumped over the moon;
The little dog laughed
To see such sport,
And the dish ran away with the spoon.

the
dish
ran away
with
the spoon

51

Bye, baby bunting,
Daddy's gone a-hunting,
Gone to get a rabbit skin
To wrap the baby bunting in.

Hickety, pickety, my black hen,
She lays eggs for gentlemen;
Gentlemen come every day
To see what my black hen doth lay.

Jack be nimble,
  Jack be quick,
Jack jump over
  The candlestick.

Sing a song of sixpence,
  A pocket full of rye;
Four and twenty blackbirds,
  Baked in a pie.

When the pie was opened,
  The birds began to sing;
Was not that a dainty dish,
  To set before the king?

The king was in his countinghouse,
  Counting out his money;
The queen was in the parlor,
  Eating bread and honey.

The maid was in the garden,
  Hanging out the clothes,
When down came a blackbird
  And pecked off her nose.

four and
twenty
blackbirds

the geese are getting fat

Christmas is coming,
  The geese are getting fat,
Please to put a penny
  In the old man's hat.
If you haven't got a penny,
  A ha'penny will do;
If you haven't got a ha'penny,
  Then God bless you!

Doctor Foster went to Gloucester
In a shower of rain;
He stepped in a puddle,
Right up to his middle,
And never went there again.

This is the house
that Jack built.

This is the malt
That lay in the house
   that Jack built.

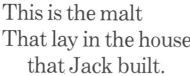

This is the rat,
That ate the malt
That lay in the house
   that Jack built.

This is the cat,
That killed the rat,
That ate the malt
That lay in the house
 that Jack built.

This is the dog,
That worried the cat,
That killed the rat,
That ate the malt
That lay in the house
 that Jack built.

This is the cow with the crumpled horn,
That tossed the dog,
That worried the cat,
That killed the rat,
That ate the malt
That lay in the house
 that Jack built.

This is the maiden all forlorn,
That milked the cow with the crumpled horn,
That tossed the dog,
That worried the cat,
That killed the rat,
That ate the malt
That lay in the house
 that Jack built.

This is the man all tattered and torn,
That kissed the maiden all forlorn,
That milked the cow with the crumpled horn,
That tossed the dog,
That worried the cat,
That killed the rat,
That ate the malt
That lay in the house
 that Jack built.

This is the priest all shaven and shorn,
That married the man all tattered and torn,
That kissed the maiden all forlorn,
That milked the cow with the crumpled horn,
That tossed the dog,
That worried the cat,
That killed the rat,
That ate the malt
That lay in the house
 that Jack built.

This is the cock that crowed in the morn,
That woke the priest all shaven and shorn,
That married the man all tattered and torn,
That kissed the maiden all forlorn,
That milked the cow with the crumpled horn,
    That tossed the dog,
    That worried the cat,
    That killed the rat,
    That ate the malt
    That lay in the house
        that Jack built.

This is the farmer sowing his corn,
That kept the cock that crowed in the morn,
That woke the priest all shaven and shorn,
That married the man all tattered and torn,
That kissed the maiden all forlorn,
That milked the cow with the crumpled horn,
            That tossed the dog,
            That worried the cat,
            That killed the rat,
            That ate the malt
            That lay in the house
                that Jack built.

This is the horse and the hound and the horn,
That belonged to the farmer sowing his corn,
That kept the cock that crowed in the morn,
That woke the priest all shaven and shorn,
That married the man all tattered and torn,
That kissed the maiden all forlorn,
    That milked the cow with the crumpled horn,
    That tossed the dog,
    That worried the cat,
    That killed the rat,
    That ate the malt
    That lay in the house
        that Jack built.

Little Miss Muffet
Sat on a tuffet,
Eating her curds and whey;
Along came a spider,
Who sat down beside her
And frightened Miss Muffet away.

Tweedledum and Tweedledee
Agreed to have a battle,
For Tweedledum, said Tweedledee,
Had spoiled his nice new rattle.
Just then flew by a monstrous crow
As big as a tar barrel,
Which frightened both the heroes so,
They both forgot their quarrel.

tweedledum
and
tweedledee

This little pig went to market,
This little pig stayed home,
This little pig had roast beef,
This little pig had none,
And this little pig cried, "Wee-wee-wee-wee-wee,"
    All the way home.

Wee Willie Winkie runs through the town,
Upstairs and downstairs in his nightgown,
Rapping at the window, crying through the lock,
"Are the children all in bed? For now it's eight o'clock."